A HARD LIFE
THE STORY OF TIP DENTON

GIACOMO GIAMMATTEO

INFERNO PUBLISHING COMPANY

© Copyright **2017** Giacomo Giammatteo

All rights reserved. No part of this book may be reproduced or transmitted in any form or by any means, electronic or mechanical, including photocopying, recording, or by any information storage and retrieval system, without written permission from the author, except for the inclusion of brief quotations in a review.

This ebook is licensed for your personal enjoyment only. This ebook may not be re-sold or given away to other people. If you would like to share this book with another person, please purchase an additional copy for each reader. If you're reading this book and did not purchase it, or it was not purchased for your use only, then please return to

INFERNO PUBLISHING COMPANY, Houston, Texas.

For more information about this book, visit the website.

Cover design by Natasha Brown

Book design by Giacomo Giammatteo

This edition was prepared by Giacomo Giammatteo gg@giacomog.com

Print ISBN 978-1-940313-42-9

Electronic ISBN978-1-940313-41-2

This book is a work of fiction. Names, characters, places, and events herein are either the product of the author's imagination or are used fictitiously. Any resemblance to actual persons, living or dead, is entirely coincidental.

ISBN: 978-1-940313-41-2

❦ Created with Vellum

TIP DENTON

Tip walked down the hall, turned left, looked around, then made his way to the graveyard. His old pal, Missy, was still manning the gates.

"What's up, Tip? Still looking for that phantom killer?"

"I'll find him some day," Tip said. "Then you won't be laughing."

"Dig up my grave when you do. I'd like to know."

Tip spent a few hours searching old files, then he called it a night. As he made his way back to his desk, he ran into his partner, Connie Gianelli.

"Tip, what are you doing here?"

"I was about to ask the same of you."

"I'm doing some late reports, but you didn't answer my question."

Tip looked around, then turned to Connie and whispered. "Looking into an old case—my mother's murder from twenty years ago."

"Twenty years ago? I think you need to tell me about it."

"I don't know," Tip said. "All the people involved with this case have had something bad happen to them. I don't want you hurt."

Houston Police Headquarters downtown

Connie grabbed his hand and tugged, heading toward the parking lot. "Now I *know* you're telling me about it. No partner of mine is sticking their neck out while mine is buried in the sand."

Connie kept hold of him until it was time to get in the car. Once inside, she said, "Start talking, Denton. I'm all ears."

HOLLY'S STORY

Holly Denton was a country girl, and she let everyone know it by always using her long Texas drawl, a drawl as long as the freeway from Austin to El Paso. She looked like a country girl, too. She sported long blonde hair that she kept in a ponytail, and she had a slim figure with big breasts that she had a penchant for showing off. And she owned a smile about half as long as her drawl, one that she loved flashing at every man who looked her way.

Holly had come to Houston about ten years ago, when she was eighteen and so far she didn't have much to show for it. A no-account job as a waitress at the House of Pies and a ten-year-old son who was nothing but trouble. Not to mention he cost a pretty penny to feed—that damn boy ate more than a pregnant sow.

Holly worked the night shift at the restaurant, but the night shift was okay with her. It gave her time to herself while the boy was in school and it made it so she didn't have to pay no babysitter. He watched TV, then went to bed. At least, that's what he was supposed to do.

House of Pies

On Friday and Saturday nights Holly took him to work and had him clean the tables. Folks seemed to like him, and they tipped him accordingly, which was fine by her. If this kept up she might start bringing him every night. Hell, one night the little shit made almost as much as she had. That kind of money she couldn't afford to ignore.

George came home from school on Friday afternoon. He opened the door and hollered, "Hey, Mama."

"Don't worry about that 'hey, Mama,' just get your ass dressed or we'll be late. Shift starts in one hour."

"Mama, it's Jake's birthday and he invited everyone over. He's having a big party."

"Ain't that a shit," Holly said. "Shame you can't go."

"What do you mean? Why not?"

"First, because I said so. And second, because you have to work and make money. Money doesn't grow on trees, you know."

"Mama, just tonight?"

"Not a chance. Jake will have a birthday next year and the one after that. Go to one of them."

"C'mon, Mama. If I don't go to his, he won't come to mine. Besides, I been meaning to ask you, when is mine?"

"I don't know."

"What do you mean, you don't know? How can you not know my birthday? You gave me birth, didn't you?"

"Just because you came out of me doesn't mean I'm here to keep track of you. If you must know, I think it was a Friday, late in March. But that's all I know. If you ask again, I'll smack you upside the head."

George nodded. He knew what that meant because he'd experienced it before. She'd smacked him upside the head more than a few times, and if Mama said she'd smack him upside the head, she meant it. George didn't want any part of that. Besides, he got what he wanted. Close enough anyway. From now on, his birthday would be the last Friday of March, no matter the date. If it was good enough for Thanksgiving, it was good enough for him.

George dropped his book bag in the corner then walked toward the bedroom. "What do you want me to wear?"

"Something nice. They tip you more when you look nice. And sure as hell we need the money."

George took off his school clothes and started putting on his work pants, a pair of blue wool slacks one of his mom's friends had bought for him. "I don't want to go tonight."

"I don't give a shit what you want. You're going."

George finished dressing then slammed his door. It was going to be another boring night at the diner.

From Holly's house, it was a forty-minute drive to the diner, and George didn't say a word the whole way. He didn't see much sense in talking, as his mother would either smack him or tell him what he said was stupid. Neither response was what he was looking for, so he kept quiet, which is what she'd have told him to do anyway.

As they drove down the freeway, he thought about how nice it would be to have a mom like Jake's. Then he silently chided himself for thinking that. George's mom fed him and clothed him; that was more than some did. At least that's what she told him.

That party probably won't be so fun anyway. Might as well go to work and earn some money.

When they arrived, Holly parked behind the diner in a spot reserved for employees. She grabbed an extra pack of Marlboros from the glove compartment and a pack of Orbit Sweet Mint gum from the console. If tonight was as busy as last Friday, she'd need both.

THE CROWD KEPT INCREASING, and by ten o'clock it proved to be a busy night even for a Friday, busier than the last week. By midnight, the place got even more crowded, people waiting in line to be seated.

Holly turned in her most recent order, then grabbed her pack of smokes and headed for the back door. "Cover for me, Sall? I'll only be a minute."

"Where do you think you're going?" Sally said.

"Have a smoke. I haven't had one in almost an hour. And from the looks of things, it'll be a while before I can again."

"All right, but you better hurry the hell up. I've got my own tables to worry about."

"Just keep fillin' the coffee cups. They're not here for the food anyway."

"Speaking of what they're here for. Look who just walked in—Mr. Big, that rugged-looking young guy who's been hitting on you."

"Shit! All right, keep him busy. I'll hurry up."

Ten minutes later, Holly came back in. She shoved a few pieces of gum in her mouth, grabbed her order pad, then walked to the seating area. She approached Mr. Big, as she and Sally had named him, smiled, and said, "What'll it be? And no smart answers, please; we're busy tonight."

"Why, Sugar, I wouldn't give a sweet young thing from...where is it you're from?"

Holly shifted her weight to the left foot. "Junction. It's out past San Antonio."

"Junction? What's it a junction of?"

Holly twisted her lips in a frown, and said, "It's the place where nowhere meets nothin', that's what. A hole in the wall put there so people can stop and piss on the way to El Paso."

He laughed. "Sounds like you scooted outta' there in a hurry."

"Not soon enough," she said. "Ended up leavin' with a belly full of trouble."

"What kind of trouble?"

Holly turned her head and gestured to George, who was placing silverware on a table he'd just cleaned. "That kind," she said. "The kind that stays with you for a lot of years."

Mr. Big looked surprised. "Are you talkin' about Tipmunk? Is he yours?"

"He's mine. But what the hell did you call him?"

He laughed. "The Tipmunk. That's what we call him. He's so damn cute—like a chipmunk—that you just have to give him a tip."

"It's a damn good thing. Those tips are what feed him some weeks."

Mr. Big grabbed her by the waist and pulled her onto his lap. He leaned close and whispered. "You know, you could change that if you were a little nicer."

Holly's inclination was to pull away but she didn't. Instead, she smiled and wiggled a little closer. "How nice would I have to be?"

"Nice enough to join me for dinner at my place on Tuesday night."

"Can't do it Tuesday, but Wednesday will work."

"Deal, he said. Write your number on the check and I'll call."

As Holly scribbled out her number, someone called from the kitchen. "Holly!"

She turned toward the sound, then back to Mr. Big. "Sorry, I've got to go. That's the boss and he sounds pissed."

"Go on, then," he said, and he smacked her lightly on the butt as she left. "I'll call next week. Be ready."

"I will," she said. "Wednesday."

Mr. Big laid a twenty and a five on the table, then got up and left, but not before leaving a note on the five.

George went to clean the table, and saw the note on paper clipped to the five-dollar bill. "The five is for Tip. The twenty is for Holly."

George shrieked and ran back to the kitchen, holding the five with a death grip. "Mom. Mom, look what he left me. Five dollars!"

Holly took the bill and looked at the note. *Tip. Not a bad name. Could be worse.* "Guess that does it, boy. From now on, your name is Tip Denton."

"Tip? That's a stupid name."

"Do you think that five dollars is stupid?"

"No. But—"

"No buts about it," Holly said. "Tip sounds better than George anyway."

DINNER WITH MR. BIG

The rest of the weekend sped by, then Monday night came and went almost as quickly. Tuesday, however, moved as slow as molasses.

Holly couldn't wait until Wednesday night, her meeting with the mysterious Mr. Big. She had learned his real name was Harold, but he liked being called Mr. Big or Mr. B, which was fine, because Harold was a name that didn't suit him. Leastwise not according to her reckoning.

She slept in late on Wednesday, then started getting ready about three o'clock. She stood in front of the closet with the door open, pondering which dress to wear. She figured he'd like one that hugged her curves, which didn't narrow the choices much, but it did boost her confidence. The way he'd looked at her the last time he was in to eat told her he was eager, like one of her daddy's hound dogs when they smelled a bitch in heat.

She wasn't in heat but she could make him think so. All it would take is a smile at the right time, mixed with a subtle wiggle. Holly had a damn nice figure and she intended to get the most out of it.

She'd have Mr. Big so worked up he'd be in danger of biting his tongue clean off. She'd just have to make sure he put it to good use before he went and did that. After all, she wouldn't have this figure forever; she might as well make use of it while she did.

She decided on a maroon skirt that hugged her body almost as tightly as a pair of spandex pants. And she knew how it showed off her figure by the outright stares she got from strangers when she wore them.

After setting the skirt on the bed, she pulled a pair of black lace panties from the drawer but then contemplated on whether to wear them. On the one hand it would be proper, the right thing to do. On the other hand, if she wasn't wearing them, he'd know, tight as that skirt was, and that would have him all but drooling. A wicked smile formed on her face as she put her panties back in the drawer. Drool it would be.

Condos on San Felipe

Mr. Big's driver, Jean-Paul, picked her up and drove her to a condo on San Felipe. Mr. Big had dinner catered—prime rib and mixed vegetables with double-stuffed baked potatoes, and a wine that was to die for.

"This is delicious," Holly said. "I don't think I've ever had a meal this good."

Mr. Big grinned. "You could eat like this every night if you want."

"Sounds mighty good. I might pull the stinger from a bee for that," she said.

"While I'd like to see you pull the stinger from a bee, I'd rather see what's under that skirt."

Holly smiled. "I thought you'd never ask."

She led him to the sofa, sat on his lap, and stroked his hair. "Tell me what you had in mind."

"Where are you from?" he asked.

"Already told you that—Junction, Texas, not that it matters."

"Why did you leave? Was it because of Tip?"

"Because it was Junction, Texas," she said, and laughed. "If you've ever been there, you'd know just what I mean."

"How old were you when you left?"

"Young," Holly said with a little exasperation. "Why all the questions?"

Mr. Big rubbed her leg with one hand and used the other to play with her hair. "Because I've got some powerful friends who would love to spend time with you. But they'd want assurances that it would be kept private. Can you do that?"

Holly looked at him as if he were nuts. "You want me to be a whore? Be with these men for money?"

"Not just money, darlin'. We're not talking about a twenty-dollar whore. We're talking big money—*damn* big money."

She seemed to settle down some at the mention of big money. "What do you mean by big money?"

"Probably $500-1,000 per night."

Holly didn't say anything at first, but her mind was working. One thousand dollars a month would pay for a lot of things. "I get pretty good tips where I am."

"I'm talking once a week, too. If you prove to be as good as I suspect, you could be looking at $4,000 per month by working one night a week. Work two nights per week and it's double that. I don't care what kind of tips you get at the diner, they ain't that much."

Now he had her interest. Four thousand a month was more than she dreamed of. *And for just doin'* that? Hell, she'd do it for free if they were good looking. And eight thousand a month, that was downright shameful.

"I don't know," she said. "What would I have to do?"

"Whatever they want," Mr. Big said. "Nothing that would hurt you, but anything...*normal*."

Holly remained silent while she considered his offer. She'd done this with other people for nothing. Why not get paid? And that kind of money wasn't chicken feed. She could get a new house, a new car, and new clothes, too.

After about five minutes, Mr. Big asked, "Well?"

"Nobody will know?"

"That's the whole point, honey. We *don't want* anyone to know. The only way someone will know is if you tell them, and if you do that it will piss us off."

She struggled with the decision, but in the end, her desire for new things won. "I guess," she said.

He smiled. "Good. Now take your clothes off and let me see what you're hiding."

A HARD LIFE

She hesitated, but then she stood and unzipped her skirt, letting it fall to the floor. She wore nothing underneath.

Mr. Big gave a long, slow whistle. "Damn, girl. You look nicer than I thought. And I love the no-panties look."

Mr. Big stood and led her to the bedroom. They took a shower, then made love. An hour later, he walked back to the living room, her trailing him.

"You can start Friday night," he said.

"I've got to work," Holly said.

Mr. Big shook his head. "Forget that. I'll make sure you don't. And you won't have to work night shift ever again. Trust me. I'll take care of it."

"But he doesn't have anybody else to—"

"Don't worry. I'll handle it. He'll just have to find somebody. It's not your problem now."

Two hours later, Jean-Paul drove her home. She didn't sleep much, thinking mostly about the proposal Mr. Big had made. She kept thinking how wrong it was to do, but then thought about how many things she could buy with the money. Shortly before daybreak, she drifted off.

A LOT TO THINK ABOUT

All day long Holly thought about her dilemma, then she mulled over her situation on the drive home. On the one hand there was her reputation. If she gave a damn about that she should say no, but she didn't have a reputation to begin with—not good or bad. So what did it matter? Besides, who would know? Sure as hell Mr. Big and his associates weren't going to go around the city bragging about slumming with a waitress.

Then there was the time involved. The more she thought about that aspect—about how little time for so much money—the more appealing it was, not a negative. She'd be getting paid for doing what she liked doing anyway, even if it wasn't with men she wanted. And that little shit kid of hers would be out of her hair one or two additional nights a week.

There was the risk for disease, though she doubted if these men were the typical transmitting type. And the hours were odd—late and unpredictable—but that didn't bother Holly. She kind of liked that part of the job.

On the positive side there was the money—and she desperately needed that. And desperately wanted it too.

From what Mr. Big had told her, she'd be making a hell of a lot for damn near nothing. It would be like getting fifty-dollar tips from every table she waited on. Holly smiled. She'd made up her mind. This was a proposal she could live with. All that was left was to talk to Sally about watching Tip. And of course, talking to Tip.

She drove a couple of miles, then thought some more. If Mr. Big was right, she wouldn't even have to work nights anymore at the diner. That would be better for Tip.

That might have been an opportune reason to justify her decision, but if it was, it was working. She felt better already.

On Monday, Holly got in early so she could talk to Sally alone. She sat next to her in a booth where Sally was drinking coffee, then signaled her outside. "I need a moment," Holly said. "Won't be long."

Sally followed her outside, pulling a cigarette out the moment they exited. "What's up?" she asked as she lit the smoke.

"I got a new job."

Sally yanked the smoke from her mouth. "What?"

"Yeah. I haven't told anybody else, not even Sam. I wanted you to be the first to know."

"Damn, Holly. Where are you going? What are you doing?"

"I ain't really going anywhere. I'm keeping this job, just adding on the other work. It'll only be a couple of nights a week, and the money is great."

"Doing what? You got room for me?"

Holly didn't need to re-evaluate to know the answer. Sally was a little on the heavy side, not the kind of figure conducive to this line of work. Besides, she doubted if Sally's religious upbringing would condone this type of activity. "I don't think they have any other openings," Holly said.

Sally put the smoke back in her mouth. "Okay, well if anything comes open, let me know. I could use the money."

"Speaking of which," Holly said. "I'll be needing somebody to watch little Tip on the nights I work. You want to do that? I can pay pretty good money—eighty per night—and you know how much he loves his Aunt Sall."

"Eighty per? What the hell kind of job did you get? How much are you making?"

"Doesn't matter what I'm making, and it doesn't matter what the job is, are you gonna watch him or not?"

Sally puffed hard on the cigarette. "I'm guessing I know what you're thinking of, and it ain't right. Ain't right for a single woman and sure as hell ain't right for a mom. Nothing good ever comes of situations like this. Tough it out. You can do it. I've been doing it for fifteen years."

"That's my point exactly," Holly said. "You've been doing this for fifteen years and it's gotten you nowhere. What motivation does that give me? I ain't about to work here the rest of my life. Besides, I might get to switch to working days."

"Working days? When am I supposed to watch him? I work nights, with the peons, in case you forgot."

"I didn't forget. You only have to watch him on nights you have off. If I have to work when you do, Tip will just have to manage on his own."

"Manage on his own? That boy can't manage on his own; he's too young."

"He's been doin' it already. Who do you think watches him while I'm working?"

"You mean you been leaving that boy by himself?"

"Where do you think he's been? I can't afford to pay anybody."

"Jesus," Sally said. "How am I gonna work and watch him, too?"

"I'm not asking you to do both. I said on your nights off. C'mon, Sall, it's a chance for me to make real money. Enough so I could move out of that shithole and get a nice place to stay. Enough to get some decent clothes. Maybe even a new car."

"That all sounds good, but in all of that chatter, I didn't hear one word about Tip. You gonna do anything for him?"

"Of course I'm gonna do something for him. I just have to get on my feet first."

"And what are you doing that is gonna earn you so much money, that you won't tell me about? Are you doing something you're not supposed to do? That's what it sounds like."

"You sound like my mother used to. It's none of your business what I'm doing. Are you gonna watch Tip or not?"

Sally sighed. "I'll watch him for a few months, but not forever. I got a life too, you know. I like Tip but if I wanted kids, I'd have had them."

Holly grinned. "Thanks. I knew I could count on you."

Sally lowered her head, shook it, and mumbled. "That's your problem, girl. You're always counting on somebody. Anybody but yourself."

"What?"

"Nothin'," Sally said. "But you better get your ass inside or Sam will have a shit fit."

"All right. Thanks. I'll bring Tip by on Friday about six. Can you fix him dinner?"

"Son of a bitch. Next thing, you'll be wanting me to change his diapers."

"It's just dinner for Christ's sake. You gotta eat anyway."

"All right. I'll make hot dogs. But don't be late. Dinner's gonna be at six sharp."

Holly smiled and patted Sally on the back. "Thanks, Sall. I appreciate it." Then she hustled inside to report for work.

After work, Holly went home and waited for Tip. When he got to the house, she called him to the kitchen. "Tip, I've got to talk with you."

"What about?"

"Mom is getting a new job, so—"

"Yeah. That's what you wanted, right?"

"Well, yeah, but I'm still going to be working the old job, at least for a little while."

"What do you mean? What am I going to do?"

"You're going to have to stay with Aunt Sally for a while."

"No way. I don't want to."

"It's only on the nights I have to work this new job. And I really don't care what you want."

"Why can't I just stay here like I always do?"

"Because I said so. Now, am I gonna have a problem with you? Or are you gonna be a big boy and help your mama?"

He shrugged. "I'll help. I guess Aunt Sally is better than most."

She tousled his hair. "That's my boy. I know you'll be good for Aunt Sally."

A FEW MORE QUESTIONS

Holly didn't take long to get ready. She purposefully neglected her panties, then selected a tight-fitting dress that was darn near see-through. It didn't much matter who she was seeing—if he had a dick, he'd like what she wore.

About six o'clock, Jean-Paul picked her up in a limo. She climbed into the back seat, not worrying about the amount of flesh she flashed. "Where are we going, Jean-Paul?"

He cleared his throat, glanced at her in the mirror, then said, "I am to drop you off at Mr. Big's. Someone else will probably take you from there."

Holly nodded. It didn't matter to her where they were going, she'd just asked to make conversation. It took about forty minutes to get to Mr. Big's place. After some small talk and a drink, they had dinner and a cup of coffee.

Afterward, Mr. Big wasted no time. He grabbed hold of her waist and pulled her toward him. "Let me have a look at that magnificent body again."

"Not yet," she said. "I have a few more questions."

"Shoot, darlin'. Ask away. I'll tell you anything you need to know."

Holly walked past him and sat on the sofa, close to his side. "What about if you set up a *meeting* and I don't like the person?"

"Don't like him how? You've got to be more specific than that. Do you mean don't like his looks? His nationality? His politics? Give me something to work with. I don't have time for prejudice or political bullshit. A dick's a dick. Take it or leave it, but don't judge it by its color."

Holly shook her head. "That's not what I'm trying to say. I mean just don't *like* him, like I don't feel good about him. Or safe."

"Ah. Now we're gettin' somewhere. If you don't feel safe, cut it off. Tell my man to take you home or bring you back to me."

"Tell your man? You mean someone will be with us the whole time?"

Mr. Big laughed. "Of course someone will be with you. You don't think I'd trust degenerates like these people with my prized honey, do you?" He slipped his hand underneath her and squeezed her butt cheeks. Then he smiled. "Don't worry about a thing. I'll take care of it all. No one is going to hurt you. I'd kill the first man who did."

"But I don't know if I want a damn audience."

He laughed. "Sweetheart, he won't be in the same room, but he'll be within shouting distance. Besides, don't worry about someone staring at your ass. People already do that. It's too pretty not to stare. And what difference does it make if they stare at it while you're naked?"

Holly let that thought bounce around in her head, then nodded. "I guess you're right."

"Of course, I'm right. Don't give it another thought." He leaned in close and kissed her. "There's only one thing I want you thinking of tonight."

Holly pulled away. "Before we get started on that, two more questions. How will I be paid? And when?"

"Now we're gettin' to the sweet part. You'll be paid in cash at the end of every night. And don't worry, these aren't the kind of men who miss payments, at least not for this type of product. Besides, if they miss a payment, the consequences would *not* be good."

"What do you mean?"

A smile flashed on his face. "Don't worry about what I mean, just know that consequences would not be good. These are smart people. They understand consequences and repercussions, so they'll be careful. Mighty careful."

She leaned back on the sofa and put her finger to her lips. She'd pretty much made up her mind, but she didn't want to tell him yet. "I'll think about it and let you know. How about Friday?"

"Friday's fine, darlin', but don't take too much time deciding. I got my fishing line cast in more than one pond."

She smiled. "Friday it is, then. I'll talk to you at dinner."

LET'S DO IT

Friday day seemed to fly on by and before she knew it, Holly was on her way home. She took a quick shower, changed into something Mr. Big hadn't seen her wear, then headed out, laying a sheet over her car seat so she didn't get dirty; she was driving herself tonight. She pulled into the parking garage at the condominiums forty-five minutes later.

Mr. Big answered the door, dressed in his favorite cashmere robe and silk-lined slippers. "Right on time," he said. "I admire punctuality."

"Im not always punctual," Holly said, "but I try not being too late."

"Since you showed up, I'm assuming you've decided to move ahead with our little venture; otherwise, you wouldn't have come."

Holly turned to look at him. "Don't think you know me so well. You might be surprised."

Mr. Big laughed. "I might be, but unless I miss my guess, you're in, right?"

"I'm in , but only for a couple of months. Just to get enough money for a new start."

"Fine with me, honey. But once you get a taste of what that money can buy, I think you'll be in for the long haul. I haven't seen anyone yet who quit on their own."

Holly knew he was right; she'd even told herself she wasn't going at this full time, that she'd be quitting once she got a base to stand on. She felt she needed that, to tell herself it this arrangement was only temporary. God forbid if her father and mother ever found out. "We'll see," she said. "For now, let's say we have an agreement."

Mr. Big laughed and grabbed a glass to pour a drink. He lifted the glass and gestured toward her. "Want one?"

"I think I will," she said, and sat in the chair. It was a Queen Anne wingback chair with floral upholstery. *Surprisingly comfortable.* She kicked her shoes off, lifted them onto a nearby Ottoman, and set her drink on the coaster sitting on the end table. "When do we start this?"

"Next week," he said. "Might as well get in one more night of fun before we put you out to pasture, so to speak."

"Sounds fine by me."

"Good. Now get a new negligé from the bedroom closet and put it on, then come back out to see me. And get rid of that one you've been wearing. It looks as if it came from a shop in the ghetto."

Holly scowled, but headed toward the bedroom as she did. "It doesn't look *that* bad."

"I guess it depends on who's doing the looking. And while we're talking about clothes, I'll have Jean-Paul pick you up tomorrow and take you shopping for a few outfits. You'll need them."

"I can't afford new outfits."

"You'll be able to soon enough. I'll front you the cost until you earn it."

"I ain't spending money on clothes until I've got plenty to spend. Besides, the clothes I got are—"

"—shit. They make you look like a slut. You need a high-class look. Something fashionable but sexy. Keep dressing like you have been and you'll get paid that way too. No more than a hundred a night. Listen to me and I'll guarantee you a minimum of five hundred, probably more. The more depends on how you perform and from what I can tell, you'll do fine in that department."

"I like the sound of that," Holly said, then she slugged the rest of her drink and held it out for a refill. She was going to need more than one to get through the night. *It will all be worth it.* At least that's what she kept telling herself.

Sometime around three o'clock she woke with Mr. Big's naked body draped over hers. She immediately began to reconsider her earlier thoughts about this being worth it, but then he stirred.

"Sorry about that," he said. "I didn't realize I'd fallen asleep."

"Roll over," she said. "I've got to get going."

He moved to the side of the bed, then sat up. "I had no protection last night. You know that, don't you?"

A twinge of guilt ran through her. "I know, but I figured—"

"—Don't figure. Insist on protection. Do *nothing* without it. It's the only way to be certain."

"Okay. Got it."

"I hope you understand. Remember what I said about consequences?"

"Yeah, I remember," Holly said.

"Your clients aren't the only ones who need to worry."

"You don't have to worry. I already have one ten-year-old problem. I don't need another, no matter whose kid he is."

Mr. Big smiled broadly. "Good. That's what I like to hear."

She got up to dress, and he said, "Don't forget, Jean-Paul will pick you up to go shopping for clothes. Expect him around ten."

She glanced at the clock, then said, "That doesn't give me much time for sleeping."

"I haven't seen the woman yet who needs much sleep in order to shop. I'm sure you'll be fine."

As it turned out, he was right about the sleep. Halfway through the lingerie section at *A Lady's Choice,* Holly forgot that she'd been up most of the night; instead, she focused on selecting some of the most gorgeous clothes she'd ever seen. Best of all, she didn't even look at the price.

Some people say that giving birth is the best experience you can have, but to Holly, a full-blown shopping spree topped that by a long shot. She'd never had more fun in her life. Aside from the thrill of getting new clothes, she didn't have to pay for them, not yet anyway.

All through the weekend, her nerves were on edge. She was anxious about Wednesday, her first day *on the job.* Mr. Big said she'd be meeting with a businessman from Tokyo, and he stressed how important it was to make the man happy. That responsibility fell on her shoulders, or on other parts of her anatomy.

She selected what she considered to be her sexiest outfit, doused herself with the best perfume, and had a friend of Sally's, a professional, apply her makeup. If she didn't wow him with this, he was not wow-able.

On the night in question, Jean-Paul picked her up shortly after six and drove her to the Four Seasons Hotel, where he escorted her to the suite on the top floor. Jean-Paul waited in living room, as instructed, while she accompanied the man to the bedroom. His name was Mr. Yamamoto.

She struggled to make conversation with Yamamoto, whose endurance proved less than satisfactory and whose command of the English language was even less satisfactory. By two o'clock, the session was over, and she and Jean-Paul were on the way home.

"Were you bored, Jean-Paul?"

"Not so much. I read whenever I have to wait like this."

"Do you do this often? Take women on liaisons, I mean."

"Occasionally. Though I doubt that he would want me to discuss details."

"I see. Perhaps you can tell me, how I stack up?"

He looked through the rearview mirror. "Looks wise...maybe the best."

"But...?"

"But your conversation and humor need work."

Holly's smile vanished, replaced by a frown.

"You asked," he said.

"No, that's all right. I needed to know. Thank you for being honest."

A BELLY FULL OF PROBLEMS

During the next six months, Holly worked hard on improving where she needed to. Her physical performance was stellar, according to her clients, but she still needed work on getting rid of her Texas drawl, and adding a bit of sophisticated humor and charm. The drawl she tried to replace with a generic American accent that hinted of *nowhere*; for the humor and charm, she solicited help from a few friends of Mr. Big.

Things were going fine; money was rolling in; she got at least two parties a week; and the feedback from her clients was nothing but positive.

A couple of times there ended up being more than one person participate, which made her payment substantially larger. And one time, the other participant was not a male. Holly didn't care. It was all green to her.

On those nights when more than one person took part, they usually celebrated until early in the morning. When that happened, Mr. Big's driver would take her home, where she would change her clothes, then drive to work. She'd be tired, but it was worth it. Besides, for a few bucks, Sally picked up the slack and let her take it easy.

The new job was going great. She had enough money to buy new clothes; hell, she even had some left over to buy clothes for Tip. Not that he needed them. The little shit never went anywhere, except with Sally on her weekly trip to the mall. He ought to feel lucky that Holly thought enough about him to waste good money on jeans and sneakers, especially as much as sneakers cost.

Another half a year passed and things got better. Holly had saved enough to move out of their dog-shit slum house and buy a new house out near Katy. It wasn't a big house, but it was new and it was comfortable, and it was in a decent neighborhood. That was more than she anticipated having when she began her *career* at the diner. She never dreamed she'd have this much.

And all because she'd been willing to spread her legs for a couple of old fools. The more thought she put into it, the more convinced she was that she'd made the right decision. Hell, it wasn't like she was some twenty-dollar whore; she was getting a thousand, or more, per night—for one session. It would be a cold day in hell before she opted to quit this job. Mr. Big might ask her to quit as she got older, but she'd let him call that shot. Sure as shit, she wasn't going to initiate the termination.

By February, money was rolling in, she had bought a new car, and Tip was even enjoying his time with Sally. Then one day at work she got sick. The next day she threw up. On the third day, she felt sick again, and started for the bathroom.

"What's up?" Sally asked. "Something wrong? You never get sick."

"Nothing," Holly said, brushing it off. "Probably ate some bad beef or something like that. Might have been that damn sausage we had this morning. It tasted kind of funny."

"I had the same sausage and it didn't bother me," Sally said. "You sure nothing's wrong?"

"Nothing's wrong. What the hell could be wrong?"

"I hate to bring this up, but you've been sick the last three days, and you said you didn't feel well last week."

"So what? I had a damn bug. Probably from that little shit Tip. He's always bringing one disease or another home from school."

"Holly, when was the last time you had your period?"

"What?"

"Your cycle, girl. When was the last time?"

"Christ, you're paranoid. I just had it ..."

"What?" Sally said.

"What's the date today?"

"The seventh."

"Son of a bitch. I should have had it on the twenty-third or so."

"Goddamn!"

"Goddamn ain't the half of it. He's gonna kill me. He warned me not to get pregnant. What the hell am I gonna do?"

Sally put her arm on Holly's shoulder. "The first thing we're gonna do is find out for real if you're pregnant or not. And I don't mean by those tests you do at home. We're gettin' you to a real doctor."

Holly begged off the sessions that Mr. Big had arranged that week, claiming to be sick. By the following Thursday, she had the doctor's report. She was indeed, pregnant.

DIFFICULT DECISIONS

After finding out she *was* pregnant, Holly had decisions to make. She realized she was going to lose her income or at least the part that mattered.

Besides, even if she had an abortion, Mr. Big would find out and cut her off. He'd never trust her again.

While trying to figure out what to do, she decided she would have an abortion and try to hide it from him. There was no way she was telling him about her condition. She figured she could be back to work in a couple of weeks and nobody would know.

MR. BIG SUSPECTED something after she called in sick the following week. He had Jean-Paul follow her to find out what was going on. Holly led him to a doctor who was well-known for abortions, and when Jean-Paul reported it to Mr. Big, he asked Holly to explain.

He called her at her house. "You have some kind of problem, Holly?" he asked.

"Nothing," she said. "I must have come down with some kind of bug or something. I've been feeling terrible."

"Based on the choice of doctor you visited, I'd venture to guess that the problem is a little more severe than a bug."

"What do you mean?" Holly asked.

"I mean, I know that doctor you visited. And before your mind begins to wonder, yes, I had you followed. And that doctor does not treat people with the flu; he practices more serious medicine."

Holly sat silent, then said, "Okay. I had an abortion. I'm sure you know that by now. But I saved the DNA, so I know who the father is. And I've got the test results hidden, so don't try anything."

Mr. Big must have panicked. This was just the type of circumstance he didn't want. "And don't try to play games with me. I want the test results, and I want *all* of the data. There can't be any proof of this lying around."

"It's not lying around. I've seen to that. I have three copies of proof, and they're hidden in places you'd never find. If you want the test results, I want money."

"Don't be a fool, Holly. You can't play this game."

"I'm already playing. And I'm winning. I want three hundred thousand dollars, all in cash. Give me that, and it goes away."

"Three hundred thousand? That's a lot of money."

"Not nearly as much as child support and inheritance would be."

"And how do I know you won't come back for more?"

"You don't know. In fact, you don't even know if the baby has been aborted. Maybe I just told you that."

"So that's the way you want to play it?"

"It's not what I *want* to do, but I have to. I can't go back to living off what a waitress earns."

"If that's all that's bothering you, I can—"

"—No. I want three hundred thousand. If not, you or one of your prominent friends will be announcing a new baby."

"I thought you had an abortion?"

"That's what you inferred. But it might not be the case."

Mr. Big waited a few seconds, then he said, "Holly, if you didn't have an abortion, you *need* to. And, you need to get rid of any resulting evidence. The people you're dealing with don't take kindly to blackmail. Punishment will amount to a lot more than a slap on the wrist."

"Ain't nobody sayin' nothing about blackmail. I'm just asking for what's fair. Nothing more. If I wanted blackmail money, I'd be asking for millions. I know who these people are; I'm not stupid, you know."

"And how do I know you're not stupid? I consider you stupid for just proposing what you did. And besides, what's to prevent you from getting the three hundred thousand and then coming back for more?"

"I wouldn't do that."

"Oh, I see. I'm supposed to accept the word of a whore and a blackmailer."

Mr. Big heard a noise like a phone dropping. She must have been shocked that he'd call her a whore. But if she thought about it, that's what she was—in a technical sense—but him calling her that must have made her face what she was.

"I'm offended," she said. "When have I given my word and broken it?"

"When you said you wouldn't get pregnant. Or did that little detail escape your memory?"

Holly didn't respond right away. She must have been wondering how to answer that. She probably had forgotten about promising not to get pregnant. "That was an accident. This won't be. Get my money, and you won't hear from me again."

"That's a lot of money. Give me a few days to look into this," Mr. Big said, "I'll get back to you by the end of the week."

BLIND AS A BAT

Monday and Tuesday went by quickly, and on Wednesday, Holly was getting ready to go out when she heard someone come in the back door. She assumed it was Tip.

"Baby, is that you? Mama needs something."

"What do you need, Mom?"

"Bring me my purse. It's probably on the kitchen table."

"It's not there. Where else would it be?"

"For God's sake, look around. It can't be far. I didn't hide the damn thing. I swear, unless it's something you want, you're blind as a bat."

Tip walked into the bedroom a moment later with his mother's purse. "You might not think you hid it, but behind the chair in the family room is a far cry from the kitchen table. Besides, bats aren't blind. You know that, don't you?"

"Of course they are," she said. "That's why their hearing is so good and they can catch all those bugs."

"Not really, Mom. They can see almost as good as people, they just use what's called *echolocation* to find mosquitoes and other insects to eat. It's the same thing dolphins use."

Holly stopped dressing and looked at him. "Where did you learn that?"

"We had a person come to class and teach us. She works giving lectures at the bat colonies."

"Bat colonies? What the hell are you talking about?"

"Bat colonies. We've got several right here in Houston. The biggest one is in Austin, but we've got two pretty big ones, too. One is near downtown, and she said it has about 250,000 bats living under the bridge." Tip seemed excited that he was teaching his mother something. "Maybe we can go some night? Nate would go if we asked him."

"Where is it?" she asked.

"Near downtown. And we'd have to be there just when it turns dark."

Holly smiled and tousled his hair. "I guess I might be able to manage that."

The smile on Tip's face stretched from ear to ear. "Really? Can we go? Can Nate come?"

"I guess he can," she said. "See if he can go tomorrow. We'll eat dinner early then head out. But just Nate. I ain't fixin' dinner for the whole damn neighborhood."

"I know. I know," Tip said, then he raced for the phone.

"And make sure all of your homework is done before we leave. Nate, too."

"You bet, Mom. Thanks." He ran toward the kitchen, then turned and popped his head back in the bedroom door. "I love you, Mom. Thanks again."

Holly smiled. As much as he was a pain in the ass on some days, it was times like this that made up for it. "Love you too, baby. And close that damn door. I don't want somebody seein' me naked."

She heard him laugh, then he said, "Nobody's here, Mom. And stop worryin' about stupid things. We got more important things to worry about, like makin' it to the bat bridge in time."

"You let me worry about gettin' there on time, young man. And don't forget to close that door," she said, then smiled. She wished she was still at the age where being seen naked *was* a laughing matter. Regardless, in a couple of days, all the worrying would be over with. Maybe then she could relax and have fun with her boy. It was about time. She'd ignored him for too long.

NATE WAS HALF AN HOUR EARLY, which was to be expected from a little kid wanting to go somewhere. They ate a couple of hot dogs each, along with chips, then headed out toward the "bat bridge" as Tip had so brilliantly named it.

They got there in plenty of time, time enough to even secure a nice spot on a grass-covered hill where they spread a blanket out to sit on. With all of those bats, they didn't have to worry about mosquitoes, which was a pleasant surprise. It was an experience people who lived in Houston didn't often get. Mosquitoes were a part of life in this part of Texas.

Right at dusk, a young lady who worked for the city announced that the bats would be making their nightly exit soon, and she reminded everyone of the rules regarding touching any bats, even if they had fallen. She then explained how bats were not blind, despite popular myth, and talked about how they did *not* get tangled in people's hair or attack people for no reason. "In fact, bats are our friends, especially here in Texas. They eat tons of insects every night, and many of them are mosquitoes. Living near a thriving bat colony is like having the world's best mosquito system."

By the time she finished talking, the bats began emerging from under the bridge by the thousands—hell, tens of thousands. They flew in large groups formed in a swirling S formation, then, when far enough away, they began spreading out to hunt. It was a scary prospect for someone who grew up thinking bats were bad, but the kids seemed to love it, and that made Holly happy.

"How do they hunt?" Nate asked.

"They mostly use a process called echolocation," the lady said. "Even though the bats can see using their eyes, they can 'see' better with their ears."

"What do you mean?" Tip asked.

"Bats have such good hearing that they send out little 'beeps' like a dolphin or a submarine. Some bats are so good at echolocation that they can detect and avoid wires as thin as human hairs. If a mosquito or a fly gets identified by one of their blips, there is a better than average chance it will be caught. It won't get away."

"So they hunt by *listening?*" Tip asked.

"Absolutely," the woman said. "They're always listening."

Tip looked over to his mother and nudged her. "Told you they weren't blind," he said.

Holly laughed. "So you did, little smart ass. Now you and Nate get yourselves ready to leave. Make sure you have everything. It's almost time to go."

They stayed for a few minutes after the bats had gone, then Holly, Tip, and Nate headed out. "That was fun, boys. I'm glad we came to see this."

"Yeah, cool, huh? Who knew bats could be so neat?" Tip said.

"I wouldn't go as far as to call them 'neat', but they're better than I originally thought. Makes you wonder what else you might be thinking wrong about."

"Like what?"

"I don't know. Like snakes and spiders, and lots of other things. People too."

Tip opened the back door to the car and got in. "What about people?"

"I don't know. Like how i've said a thousand times that rich people weren't nice. Well, it's not true. Maybe it's just that rich people I've met haven't been nice. I'm sure there are rich people that are very nice. Just like I'm sure that there are rich people who tell their kids that poor people are not nice. Truth is, neither one of us is right or wrong. There are nice rich people and not-so-nice rich people, just like there are nice poor people and not-so-nice poor people. Gives you something to think about is all."

"That's pretty cool, Mom. So the bats taught you something, huh?"

Holly laughed. "I might not go that far, but yeah, I did learn something from watching the bats, so I guess you're right—they taught me something."

"That's good, Mom. Now that you know that, Nate and me can take you lots of places."

"You mean Nate and I, don't you?"

"No, I meant me and Nate can take *you,* but if you and Nate want to take me, that's okay, too."

Holly laughed. "I give up. I guess I wasn't made to be a teacher."

"No way," Tip said. "You were made to be a mom, and you're a good one, too."

Holly smiled. *Not much was better than this.*

FISH OR CUT BAIT

*H*olly was on pins and needles all week, worried about her negotiations.

On Friday, Mr. Big called. "It's time to fish or cut bait, girl."

"What the hell are you talking about?"

"I'm talking about you moving on with your blackmail and facing the consequences or backing off and going back to waiting tables."

"I know I'm not going back to waiting tables. And if you think you frighten me by mentioning *consequences*, you're dead wrong. I've got proof, and you'll never find it."

"It's not a good idea to threaten me," Mr. Big said. "If I have a mind to find your evidence, I will. No matter where it is. Remember, I don't need to find where you stashed your papers. If the paperwork from the lab disappears, your copy isn't worth shit."

"I'll take my chances. Will you? Will they?"

"Smart girl," he said. "I guess I'll have to speak to them. I'll let them know where things stand and see what they say."

"You do that," Holly said. "I'll be waiting."

Two days later he called back. "My associates have an offer, and it's one I suggest you take. I spoke to all of them. It seems like they are reluctant to risk negative publicity, but they also feel that the amount you are asking for is too much. They agreed you should be paid something, and are willing to chip in and compensate you but *not* for $300,000. They are okay with $200,000, though and it will be all cash."

Holly didn't say anything, trying to determine if this was negotiable or if it was final.

After a long pause, Mr. Big said, "All right, young lady. It's time. Either do this or take your chances."

"Two-fifty and you have a deal," she said.

She waited through the silence, holding her breath until he said, "Deal."

A surge of excitement coursed Holly's veins. "Great. You won't regret it. This will get things over with once and for all. How do you want to do this?"

"It's still going to take me a few days to get the cash together. I'll send someone over on Thursday with a bag. Have the evidence with you. And don't hold out on me. I want it all. I don't want you coming back to me in a year and saying you want more."

"You don't have to worry about that. I'm not greedy—just needy."

Mr. Big hung up the phone and punched the wall beside him. *Damn girl. Why'd she have to go and get greedy?*

He poured himself a drink, even though it was far too early, and pondered his situation. For ten or fifteen minutes he thought about it, then decided.

"Jean-Paul!"

A moment later, Jean-Paul walked in. "Yes, sir?"

"Get Mr. Sebastian on the phone. Tell him I have a job for him."

"Yes, sir."

SOMETIME AROUND SEVEN O'CLOCK, Mr. Sebastian arrived.

He went to the kitchen, poured himself a drink, then sat in a chair beside the sofa. "You asked to see me?"

Mr. Big nodded. "I need a job done. An assignment for your nameless friend."

"He's expensive. Are you sure someone else can't do it?"

Mr. Big shook his head. "I need more than a standard job. I need some evidence retrieved. He'll have to meet her."

"That's no problem."

"I don't want him swayed. She's a good-looking woman. Sexy as hell."

"As I said, *no problem.*"

"Just saying. I don't want his dick getting hard and messing up the job. He needs to get it done and get it done quickly."

"I'll say it one more time, *no problem.*"

Mr. Big reached to the coffee table and handed Mr. Sebastian a folder. "All the information is in here. Make sure it's destroyed when you're done."

"I know how to do my job."

Mr. Big nodded. "I know. That's why you get repeat business. I'm just nervous about this one and I can't have any mistakes."

"There won't be any."

"One more thing. I need this done on Thursday. Will that be a problem?"

"I'll check, but I doubt it."

"I guess we're done then," Mr. Big said. "I've got nothing else if you don't."

Holly pulled into a spot behind the diner, and turned the key to shut the engine off. It had been a long drive in, and she felt as if she needed a smoke, though she had quit two months ago. Hadn't had a single drag since.

She was just about to get out when the passenger door opened and a strange man got in.

"What the hell do you want?" she screamed.

"A conversation is all. Mr. Big sent me."

She smiled, feeling safer already. "Thank God. You frightened me."

He grinned. "I'm not *that* scary, am I?"

Holly laughed. "Of course not. You just startled me. I wasn't expecting you."

"Mr. Big didn't tell you I'd be coming?"

"No, he did, it's just...I didn't know when."

"Well now you know. Get the evidence and I'll get the cash." He opened the door and got out. "Be right back."

In about two minutes, he returned, satchel in hand, and got back in the front seat. "You got the evidence?"

She handed him a manila envelope. "Right here," she said. "I assume that's the cash."

"There's a whole lot of cash in here," he said, and opened the top to show her. The satchel was filled with twenties and fifties. "I need to know first if this is all of it. Are there any other papers?"

"Before I answer that, I need to count the money."

"I'm afraid this is not your money. It's mine."

"What do you mean, *yours?*

"It's what Mr. Big paid me to kill you."

Holly reached for the door, but he grabbed her. "You see, I don't really need the evidence. It would be nice if you had it, but I've got the originals."

Holly furrowed her brow and looked over at him. "That's impossible."

"Not really. We found the lab that did the work. C'mon, Holly. This is new stuff. There aren't many places that even do DNA testing and most of the places that do it require either a doctor's prescription or a pocketful of money. I doubt that you had either one of them. That left only one place, and it didn't take much juice from Mr. Big to persuade them to release your test. Now you have no original to refer back to."

"I have my copies."

He laughed. "And that's all they are—copies. Not worth the paper they're printed on, so to speak, and certainly not worth a few hundred thousand."

"You can't do this," Holly said. "We had a deal."

"Yes, and it's my understanding that the deal was for you *not* to get pregnant."

Holly was getting scared. "All right. Forget the money. Take the evidence and go."

"I'm afraid I can't do that," he said, and pulled a gun from his coat pocket. "I promised Mr. Big to do a job. Now I've got to do it."

He pulled the trigger twice. The gun was silenced so nothing was heard other than a popping sound.

He took the envelope, put it in the satchel, and wiped the car clean. He didn't think he had touched anything, but it never hurt to be sure. He thought about leaving the scene clean, but at the last minute, he slipped his signature badge under her slumped body. Now they'd know *who* did the killing, but they'd still be left to wonder why.

A GRUESOME DISCOVERY

Sally took the order from table three and looked at her watch. It was fifteen minutes past and Holly still hadn't showed.

I wonder if she's okay.

She gave the order to Sam, waited on one of her own tables, then went out back to check. With a few glances, she spotted her, leaning against the wheel of her car. *Damn girl. Probably up all night again. And I thought those days were over*

Sally marched across the parking lot calling Holly's name. "Holly, get up. Holly, get your ass up! You can't afford to be dozing off. Sam is gonna have your butt"

She was still twenty feet away from the car when she noticed the odd position Holly's body was in. She was slumped over the steering wheel as if she'd had a heart attack. Sally started running. "Holly! Holly, are you all right?" By the time Sally had taken a few steps, it was obvious Holly was not all right, and when Sally reached the car, the blood splatter was visible.

"Holly!" Sally reached for the door handle and yanked it open. Holly didn't move, her head planted in the steering wheel as if she'd been shoved in there.

Sally grabbed her collar and shook. Her head was heavy, too heavy. Another not-so-good sign. "Oh my God, baby, what have you done? What did you get yourself into?"

When Sally realized the situation, she turned and ran back to the diner. "Sam! Sam, call an ambulance. Call the police. I think somebody's killed Holly."

Sam left the eggs cooking on the griddle and ran over. "What? Where? What happened?"

"Outside," Sally said. "I don't know what happened, but I think she's dead. Good God, I think she is. Call the cops!"

On the way out the back door, Sam called 9–1–1. The dispatcher said they would send an ambulance and a police car.

"Hurry," Sam said. "Take me to her car, but don't touch anything, even if you already did. The cops are on the way. Ambulance too."

The ambulance arrived first, but as Sally had suspected, Holly was already dead. In another couple of minutes, the police came, two cars pulling up within a few seconds of each other. They were followed by a third car with two detectives—Richardson and Simms.

The detectives parked a few spaces away and got out of the car. One of the ambulance crew was shaking his head, indicating she was gone. Richardson nodded, then walked to the car, putting on a pair of latex gloves as he did. Simms had hers on and held two evidence bags in her left hand.

"Who found the body?" Simms asked.

Sally took a step forward and spoke quietly and slowly. "I did. She was late, so I came out here to look for her."

"And you found her like this? Did you touch anything?"

"I opened the door. And I shook her by the collar. That's all."

"Okay," Richardson said. He nodded to the crime scene crew who was just showing up. "They're gonna need your prints for comparison. Did you see anyone? Hear anything?"

Sally shook her head. "Nothing."

"Was she having any trouble with anyone? A boyfriend, husband? Anybody?"

Sally started to say no, then stopped. "There was one guy she was seeing. I don't know his name, but we called him Mr. Big. He used to come in here four or five times a week, but I haven't seen him since he started going out with Holly. And..."

"And what?"

"I think she'd been pregnant. I say been because I don't think she was anymore."

"Think? Do you know? Was she or not?"

"I'm not sure. She was sick a lot a little while ago, like she might've been. Then she stopped being sick, but this was after she took off for a week. Like maybe she had an abortion."

Simms nodded. "I'm sure the M.E. will tell us. If she had an abortion, he'll know."

"But she didn't have a baby?" Richardson said.

"Oh God no," Sally said. "If she was pregnant, she wasn't far along—maybe a couple of months."

"Okay," Simms said. "Leave your name and number with the uniformed officer. We'll call if we have any more questions."

"You didn't ask much," Richardson said.

"Let's have a look at the body first. That might spur more questions."

Richardson carefully opened the door and looked inside. He didn't want to disturb anything, as the crime scene crew had not yet processed the area. But what he did see was telling. "Simms, get over here."

She walked over in a hurry. "What?"

"You think this might spur a few questions?" he said, and gestured to a badge sitting on Holly's lap. It was the badge of a Texas Ranger.

"Son of a bitch," Simms said. "That'll generate more than a few questions. What the hell is that doing here?"

"Exactly," Richardson said. "That's what we need to find out."

SCENE OF THE CRIME

Richardson and Simms waited until no one was looking, then Simms stood watch while he picked up the badge. The captain had told everyone about the Ranger: if they found a body with the Ranger's signature badge, they were to keep quiet about it.

Richardson handed the badge to Simms, who placed it in an evidence bag. "What are we going to do with this?" she asked.

"Give it to the captain, who will probably hide it for some reason."

"What do you mean? Why not put it in the report?"

"Because the captain said not to, that's why."

"That's no goddamn reason."

"Enough reason for me," Richardson said. "I'm not gonna be the one to fuck things up."

Simms looked around the scene without touching anything. "What do you know about the badge?"

"Nothin' much. This must be the fifth or sixth body we've found with the badge either on it or under it. Nobody knows a damn thing about it or who's doing it. But before this body, it's been high rollers. People with money or power. At least that's the way I remember it."

"So what's a waitress at the House of Pies have in common with people that have money or power?"

"I don't know," Richardson said. "But let's not forget it's a waitress who until recently was supposedly pregnant."

Simms nodded. "There is that. I was thinking the same thing. Can't be a coincidence, especially if she had an abortion. *Somebody* wanted that baby out of the way."

"And from the looks of it, they wanted every bit of evidence out of the way."

"Then I'd say we need to find out who Mr. Big is," Simms said.

"And I'd say we better do our job and report this to the captain."

"Our job is to find out who killed this woman."

"Not so. Our job is to do what the captain tells us to do, and his instructions were explicit—if you find a body with a badge, let him know about it and don't put it in the report. Do what you want, but I'm doing what I was told."

"And I'm doing what I signed on to do—solve crimes, regardless of what the captain says."

"Go against him and it'll be your ass, Simms."

"And if I go along with him it'll be my soul. I can't live with that. I became a cop to bring criminals to justice, not let them hide in the shadows."

"Suit yourself," Richardson said. "But my report isn't going to mention a thing about a badge. This will show a mugging gone bad, that's all."

"How do you sleep, Richardson?"

"Like a baby."

Simms scowled. "If I remember right, babies cry a lot when they sleep."

"Some do. Some don't," Richardson said. "I don't."

S IMMS GOT IN EARLY, and by 8:00 had put the finishing touches on her flyer.

> If you saw *anything* relating to the murder of Holly Denton—the waitress who was killed at the House of Pies—please call Detective Laura Simms at (281) 555–6162. All replies will remain confidential.

She took the flyer to her admin and asked her to make one hundred copies. Afterward, she drove to the diner and placed them on the windshields of parked cars and set them on the counter by the cashier. With any luck, *somebody* would call.

She repeated the windshield campaign every day, placing the flyers by six in the morning and again by six at night. She also made sure the cashiers mentioned Laura's request for help to everyone, and that they handed out flyers. Simms reminded them that it was Holly, a co-worker, who was killed.

AN UNPLEASANT JOB

It's never easy to tell someone that a loved one died. When it's a little kid, it made it all the more difficult. Holly had never been the best of mothers, but it didn't matter; she was Tip's mother. And losing her would hurt him just like losing a mother would hurt any kid. Maybe more. She was all he had. He didn't have a father; he didn't have siblings; he didn't even have a dog. Sally started crying. How was she going to tell him?

She was sitting at the kitchen table drinking tea when Tip came home from school. He burst into the back door wearing a smile as wide as the stretch of road from San Antonio to Laredo.

"Aunt Sally, I'm going to Duncan's house to play. We're going to the woods."

"Have a seat, Tip. I need to talk with you."

"What about?"

"Just sit. Do you want any tea?"

Tip pulled a chair out and plopped down next to Sally. "I don't want tea. Just tell me what you want. I told Duncan I'd be right over."

Sally picked up her cup and took a long sip before setting it back down. "Tip, there was an accident at work. A bad one."

"What kind of accident? Did someone get burned?"

Sally burst into tears again. She reached over and hugged Tip, pulling him to her. "Tip, baby, your mama is dead. She's done been killed."

Tip tried yanking away but Sally held him tightly. "No. No way. She can't be. She just *can't* be."

Sally wiped tears from her eyes and tried controlling the sobs. "Honey, she is. I know how it hurts, but it's true. Aunt Sally was there when the ambulance came. They checked her."

Tip was crying now. "But how? What happened?"

"Somebody shot her, baby. Right in the car in the parking lot behind the diner. She never even got to work."

"Why? Why would anyone do that to Mom?"

Sally squeezed him and patted his back. "I don't know, darlin'. But I'm sure the police will find the person who did this. Don't worry. Aunt Sally will take care of everything. It will be all right."

"But what am I gonna do? Where will I live?" Tip was crying uncontrollably now.

"Shh. Don't worry. You can live with Aunt Sall. We'll figure it out."

Tip was sitting in the chair, his head hung low. He was crying, tears running down his face. "I don't understand. Why would anybody do this? Why would they kill Mom?"

Sally wrapped her arms around him again. "Don't you worry, sweetheart. We'll find out why."

Tip fell asleep that night on the couch. He was still crying.

LOOKING FOR A WITNESS

*S*imms' hard work paid off on day six with an early-morning anonymous call. "Detective Simms, I saw what happened. I'm willing to tell you but I don't want to get involved."

Simms glanced at her phone, but the caller ID read 'unknown caller'. That meant it was either a burner or he was hiding his ID. "That's fine," she said. "We can do this anonymously. If you want to tell me more later on, you can."

"There was a guy in a blue pickup who got out of his car and into hers. He looked to be talking to her for a while, then he must have shot her, because she slumped over on the steering wheel."

"Did you hear the shots? How many were there?"

"I didn't hear anything, but I did have my windows rolled up. It was already hot. And I had the A/C running, so it was making noise."

"Why didn't you call the cops when you saw her slump over?" Simms asked.

"I don't have no goddamn phone to do that with. And I sure as hell wasn't getting out of the car after seeing him kill her. Or at least shoot her. I ain't nuts."

"What were you doing in the car? What made you notice her?"

"I was gettin' ready to go eat breakfast. I go there every day."

"Why there? Do you live nearby?"

"Look, I'm talkin' to you because I want to help, but I ain't getting my name out there so this guy can see. This has got to stay quiet. Agreed?"

"I'll keep it quiet. I promise."

The guy was silent. He seemed to be hesitating to Simms, but then he continued. "I go there because I kinda like Holly or liked. She was cute and seemed nice. That's what made me watch her that day; she was sitting in the car when I pulled in. I knew it was her, because I know her car. Then I saw this other guy walk over and open her car door, so I stayed and watched."

"What did the guy look like? Can you describe him?"

"White. Medium height, maybe 5' 10" or 11". Slim. Brown or black hair, cut short. Sort of like a Brad Pitt haircut, but he didn't look as good as Brad Pitt."

"Good. That helps. How about age?"

"Maybe late twenties or early thirties. Could have been more or less, but I doubt it. I'm pretty good at judging age."

"That's a good description, sir. Are you sure about this?"

"I'm pretty good at noticing things about people. I've been a salesman for fifteen years. It helps to remember faces in that job."

Simms wrote it all down. "What about the vehicle? You said it was a blue pickup? What else can you tell me?"

"Not much. I'm not very good with cars. Get much past car, van, or truck, and what color it was, and I'm lost. I have no idea if it was a

Chevy or a Ford or what year it was. I can tell you it was full size, though. Not a short-bed type."

"Do you think you could recognize the man if you saw him again?"

"Maybe, but I doubt it. Leastwise, not enough to swear it was him. He was too far away."

"Okay, thanks, Mr....?"

"I told you. You ain't gettin' my name. I'll call you next week to see if you have any more questions. That's the best I'll do."

"Okay, sir. Thank you."

Simms hung up the phone, then went to see if Richardson was in yet. He was at his desk. "You file that report yet?" she asked.

"I was just about to. Why?"

"I talked to a guy who might have something for us. In fact, it might be a lead on the Ranger himself. A vehicle and a description."

"Are you serious?"

"I'm serious. You in?"

Richardson crumpled the paper he'd been typing and threw it in the trash. "Shit. Might as well go down swinging," he said. "I never liked covering things up anyway."

Simms and Richardson filed a generic report, then went out for coffee so they could talk uninterrupted. "Tell me what you've got," Richardson said.

"Not much," Simms said, "but maybe something. We've got a witness to the shooting, and he saw the guy, even though it was from a distance. Better yet, he said the guy was driving a blue pickup. He didn't know the make or model, but he said it was light blue and it was full size, not a short bed."

"I think we need to revisit the House of Pies," Richardson said. "Let's see if we can identify this witness from what we know and also see if anyone recognizes the pickup."

THE NEXT MORNING, Simms and Richardson arrived at the House of Pies early, at least early for them.

"There she is," Simms said, pointing out Sally.

Richardson sat at a booth near the front, and he was soon joined by Simms. "Might as well get coffee," he said.

Sally stopped by a moment later. "Morning, Detectives. I didn't expect to see you again. At least not this soon."

"Cases don't usually get solved so quickly," Simms said.

Sally nodded. "I guess not. Anything new?"

"That's what we're here to determine," Richardson said. "We're interested in a guy around thirty-five based on how long he said he's been a salesman, and he probably came in here for breakfast every morning. I'm guessing he sat in Holly's area or paid special attention to her."

It didn't take Sally long to think. "That would be Jake Mercer," she said. "He was in every day before seven and some days he'd stop back again in late morning for coffee and dessert. Nice guy." Sally shifted her stance and looked quizzically at the detectives. "You don't think Jake had anything to do with this, do you?"

"Should I?"

"No. No way. I was just askin'. Jake's a nice guy. Always pleasant. Very talkative. I couldn't imaging he would have anything to do with it, but I was just askin'. You can't be too careful."

"You're right about that," Simms said. "Just when you think you know someone, they surprise you."

"What are you askin' about Jake for?"

"No reason. We're trying to identify any customers who were here on a regular basis and who might have known Holly."

Sally nodded. "I see. Well, Jake would surely fit that bill. If I think of any others, I'll let you know."

"Any of them drive a light blue pickup?" Richardson asked.

Sally shook her head. "No idea. I don't see what kind of cars most people drive, though, so that don't mean much. Once they walk through the front door, they could be homeless or the goddamn mayor, and I wouldn't know the difference. Wouldn't care either."

"That's a good attitude to have. If more people lived their lives that way, we'd be better off."

"We get all kinds come in here, from the poor slob who can barely afford a cheap breakfast, to the guy who wipes his ass with twenty dollar bills. But they all get treated the same—they all get served a hot meal and bad coffee."

Richardson laughed. "I can attest to the bad coffee statement. I've eaten here before."

"Who do you think did it?" Simms asked. "Got any ideas?"

"I got no idea. She was runnin' around with a bad bunch of late, and..."

"And what?"

"I just thought of one guy who might know. He was one of them rich ones I talked about. Used to come in here quite a bit. I know Holly was mixed up with him for a while, but then she quit."

"Does he still come in here?" Simms asked.

"Not for a while. Two or three months, I'd say. Maybe more."

"You know who—"

Sally was already shaking her head. "Don't know him, or what he drives. Can't much describe him either, other than to tell you he's about forty, well off, and kinda big, maybe 6' 2", or more."

"White, black? Slim, heavy"

"White. Medium weight, maybe two hundred twenty. Brown hair, full head, too. Not balding. Good teeth."

"Good teeth?"

"Yeah. I notice things like that. When he smiled, his teeth showed nice and white. He wasn't no meth head."

Richardson handed her a card. "Call us if you see him in here again. It doesn't matter what time it is, day or night."

"I hope you mean that, because he used to come in here during night shift, after midnight."

"We both mean it, Simms said, handing her a card also. "If you don't get one of us, try the other."

Simms and Richardson asked Sally a few more questions, then they left.

"What do you think?" Richardson asked as they walked out the door.

"I think whoever wanted her dead wasn't the same guy who was driving that pickup. My guess is he was a pro doing an assignment."

"Like the Ranger?" Richardson said.

"Exactly," Simms said. "But if that was him, maybe that same blue pickup was spotted at some of the other jobs, and just maybe we'll get lucky enough to find someone who could give us a better ID."

"I doubt if we'll get that lucky, but it's worth trying."

"Either way, we've got enough to file a report now."

Richardson shook his head. "I wouldn't go that far. Not yet."

"You can't be serious?" Simms said.

"Dead serious. You haven't been here as long as I have. Politics can be brutal, and it can cost you your job."

Despite Richardson's warning, Simms filed her report. Three weeks later, she was reassigned to the Fourth Ward as a patrol officer. Richardson stayed where he was, but only after extensive interrogation regarding the case. He pled ignorance of Simms' report, and her claim of a Ranger badge being left at the scene. It seemed the way to go for him.

A NEW DIRECTION

*L*ife with Aunt Sally went fine, though it was a big adjustment. The bigger problem was school. Somehow, the kids found out about his mother, and they were brutal, calling his mother a whore and a prostitute. Tip responded to each comment with ferocity, defending his mother's honor. Because of that, it didn't take long for Tip to develop a reputation for fighting.

The rumors wouldn't quit, though, and Tip ended up fighting his way through sixth and seventh grade, all the while increasing his proficiency in the art of street fighting. Suspensions from school were frequent and, by ninth grade, he had been expelled with no chance for reinstatement. He got reinstated with help from one of Aunt Sally's friends, but the favor was a lot to ask, and it would only work once.

ON THE HOME FRONT, Sally was getting older and unable to deal with the increased supervision Tip needed. One night before he went out, she sat him down to talk. "I can't do it anymore, Tip. Much as I'd like to, and as much as I'm sure you want me to, I can't spend the energy or the money keeping you out of trouble. You're making it too tough to manage. Despite what I feel for you, I just can't manage it."

"Okay, Aunt Sall. I'll be good. I promise. No more fighting."

"You promise?"

"I promise."

Two weeks went by with no trouble, then, on a Wednesday, when Tip was changing classes, he saw a young girl near the stairs, crying. It was a girl he knew—Shirley Markus. "Shirley, what's wrong? Are you okay?"

"I'm fine. Don't worry."

"What happened? Did somebody hurt you?"

She sobbed some, then said, "It was Hap and his boys. They were saying mean things about me. Things that weren't true," she said.

Tip gritted his teeth, then said, "I'll get them for this, Shirley. Don't worry about it. It won't happen again."

Shirley grabbed his arm, and said, "No. Don't get involved, Tip. It's Hap. And he's trouble."

Two days later, Tip passed by Hap's friend, Justin, in the hall. He grabbed his collar and shoved him against the wall. "Say anything about Shirley again, and I'll kick your ass. Got that?"

"What's up, Denton? Got a thing for whores?"

That set Tip off, and he slammed Justin's head against the wall, then pummeled him with his fists. Most of the punches were body shots, but a few were aimed at Justin's nose and mouth. The third punch to the face broke Justin's nose, drawing a stream of blood that made it look worse than it was.

Within a few seconds, a crowd had gathered, and they were cheering on the combatants.

"Hit him, Tip."

"Fight back, Justin."

A moment later, someone yelled, "Teacher." And everyone scattered, including Justin.

By the end of the week, everybody was talking about the fight that was going to go down between Tip and Hap. People were even placing bets on who would win, and odds were favoring Hap. But Friday came and went and nothing happened.

Tip went to school on Monday morning, riding in with Nate as usual, but as he and Nate crossed the parking lot, he heard the unmistakable cry of a cat. When he looked to where the sound had come from, he saw Hap and a group of five or six guys standing in a circle around Palmer's pickup truck.

Tip had a feeling he knew what they were doing. "Be right back," he said to Nate.

When he got close to the back of the truck he saw a cat, a beautiful bob-tailed calico, lying in the bed of the truck. It appeared to be unconscious. He'd heard about this sick game. People would grab a cat by the neck and choke it until it passed out. Sometimes, if choked too much, the cat died, but the object was to choke it just enough to make it pass out. It was a sick game.

"Let the cat go," Tip said.

Hap stepped forward. "Well if it ain't the defender of pussies—Tip Denton."

Tip looked up at Hap. He almost lost his temper, but then remembered his promise to Aunt Sally. Instead of fighting, he ignored Hap and reached for the cat. He wasn't leaving without helping the cat.

Just as he was about to grab hold of the cat, he heard Hap yell. "Don't touch that cat. Back off."

Tip turned to him and even swallowed a little pride. "Hap, I don't want any trouble, but I'm not letting ya'll hurt this cat. It didn't do anything to you."

"None of your business what that cat did," Hap said. "It's not yours."

Tip turned to face him and stood tall. "It doesn't make any difference what this cat did, or who owns it, you don't do that to *any* animal, not you or anybody."

Noise started from the group. "Kick his ass, Hap."

"Don't let him get away with that shit."

"Punish him."

Hap cocked his arm back and took a swing at Tip's head. Tip easily ducked it, then connected with a solid right to Hap's gut, doubling him over. He followed with two lefts to the other side, bringing loud gasps from Hap.

Hap caught his breath and tried another swing from the right. Tip ducked again, but this time Hap was guarding his stomach, so Tip countered with a combination to Hap's jaw. The right sent him reeling and the left knocked him down. Hap's head hit the parking lot surface and knocked him cold.

He didn't move for more than thirty seconds despite repeated shaking. "Son of a bitch," one of his cronies said. "He's dead."

"He's not dead," another one said. "Tip just kicked his ass."

A moment later, Hap stirred, then started to get up.

"Teacher!" somebody said, and the rest of the group scattered—even Hap—leaving Tip and Nate alone.

A HARD LIFE

Mrs. Norbert walked up, grabbed Tip by the collar. "Let's go, young man. I'm sure the vice principal will want to speak to you."

"They were trying to hurt that cat," Tip said, gesturing toward the truck.

"I don't care what they were trying to do," Mrs. Norbert said, "It's no reason for fighting."

As expected, the incident resulted in Tip being expelled—again—and this time, Sally's friend couldn't get him back in.

That night, after dinner, Sally sat and talked with him. "If you don't straighten up, you'll never get in college. It might already be too late. They don't want no troublemakers at college."

"Who says I want to go to college?" Tip said. "I can get a job with Nate's uncle. Construction pays good. Besides, I could probably start right now. I'd be making good money by the time I was supposed to start college."

"And how good is it gonna pay when your knees give out? Or your back? Or when it rains and you can't work?"

"Don't worry about it, Aunt Sall. Things will be fine."

She lowered her head. Tears formed. "I've been trying, Tip. I made a vow to help you when your mama died, but you don't make it easy. I know it ain't been easy for you either, but sometimes that's the way life is. It just isn't fair, but nobody said it would be. I know your mama taught you that."

Tip walked over and hugged her. He hated to see a woman cry, especially Aunt Sall. "I'm sorry. I promise Aunt Sall. I won't do anything bad again."

"You told me that before, Tip. And look where we are now."

She shook her head while crying. "You're gonna have to go, Tip. I can't do it anymore."

Tip walked to the sink and filled the teapot with water, then he placed it on the burner. "You want tea, Aunt Sall?"

She shook her head.

"Listen," he said. "I know things haven't been easy, but it's gonna be better. I'm getting that job with Nate's uncle, and I'll pay you each week. It'll keep me out of trouble, and it will bring extra money in. What do you say? Try it out for two months and see how it works. Deal?"

"I don't know, Tip."

"C'mon, Aunt Sall. You know you want to. You could use the extra money, and you'd miss all the chores I do around here."

She laughed through her tears. "All right. Two months. But if it don't—"

Tip finished scooping sugar into his tea, then hugged her again. "It'll work, Aunt Sall. I swear."

UNIVERSAL FIX

And for almost two years it did work. Tip got up at five a.m. six days a week and came home around six p.m., after a long day at the construction site. He was typically sweaty and always dirty, but the money was good and the hard work built muscles. Overall, he was pleased.

Then everything changed. Tip was working a job building a new wing for a hospital. The rest of the crew began whistling and hollering at a young woman walking across the parking lot. Tip joined in at first, but then he recognized her as a girl from school, so he asked the guys to stop. "I know that girl," he said. "Why don't you let off. She's a nice kid."

"She's a nice kid with a nice ass," Mack said.

"Let it alone," Tip said.

Mack laughed and whistled real loud. "Hey sweetie, come on over here and spread your legs; it's lunchtime."

Tip punched him hard. Mack went down, but quickly got up. They traded a few punches, then Tip hit him cleanly with a hard right hook.

Mack went down again, but this time he hit his head on a pipe that was on the ground behind him. Blood spewed from the back on his head and pooled on the ground.

Tip reached to help him up but he was unconscious. "Shit. Give me a hand," he hollered to the other guys standing there.

They got Mack up but he was still out cold. One of the guys ran to the main section of the hospital and got help. Mack required stitches in his head, and he was admitted for a mild concussion.

Before long the police arrived. Officer Langston approached Tip. "You the one that was doing the fighting?"

"I was one of them," Tip said.

"What happened?"

Tip told him how things started and Langston nodded. "Can't say I blame you. On the other hand, you look like you've been working construction for a while now. You should know how these things go. These guys are going to yell at anything that walks by, and some of what they say will be vulgar."

"Don't make it right," Tip said. "I like to look at a pretty woman as much as anyone, but it isn't a reason to be rude."

"I agree. Come on," Langston said. "Get a cup of coffee with me."

While they drank coffee, Langston probed Tip's plans for the future, then asked if he ever thought about becoming a policeman. "It's not bad work," Langston said. "Pays decent. Benefits are good. Makes you feel good when you go home at night, and besides, we could use people like you in the department."

"I don't know," Tip said.

Langston handed Tip a card. "Think about it. Call me if you want to talk it over."

Tip went back to the hospital to make sure Mack was okay, then

A HARD LIFE

drove home, giving thought to Langston's proposal the whole way. He had never thought about being a cop, but it did have appeal—mostly that he might be able to get help on figuring out who killed his mom.

By the time he got home, he decided he would definitely quit construction, but he wouldn't go into the police force. He was going to join the Army instead.

Six months afterward, nineteen-year-old Tip Denton was inducted into the Army. Three years later he joined the special forces, and twelve months after that, he left the army a different man. He was physically hardened and mentally disciplined. And during his time in the service, he continued to send money to Aunt Sally to help her pay bills. He had also made up his mind that he was going to join the police force.

A week after he got out, Tip called Langston. "This is Tip Denton. About four years ago you gave me your card and said if I ever wanted to get in the department to call."

"I remember," Langston said. "The construction guy, right?"

"That'd be me. I've been in the Army. Now, I'm thinking I want to join the force."

"Glad to hear it," Langston said. "Meet me Friday morning for coffee at the Starbucks across from Willowbrook Mall. Eight o'clock. In the meantime, I'll make a few calls to get things rolling."

It took two months to get things going, but then Tip joined the academy. Six months after joining, he graduated as Officer Denton. He had struggled with the academic portions of the tests, but he aced the physical part.

His first assignment was patrolling the Fourth Ward, and he soon found out he had a natural rapport with the kids—good ones and bad.

It took fewer than six months for Tip to work up enough favors to earn him a night alone in the graveyard, which is what they called the cold-case files. People had warned him against trying to stir the pot, but he ignored them.

On Thursday, after his shift was over, he went to the graveyard. Missy was the admin in charge, and she had been briefed to let him in. After a few hours of searching, Tip found what he was looking for—the folder on Holly Denton.

His gut was aching from the tension and excitement, but he found the nerve to open it after a few seconds that felt like forever. Inside he found nothing—nothing but a folder stuffed with empty pages. Blank paper. He shuffled through the papers frantically, but they were all the same—empty. Somebody had removed the reports, but who would do that? And why?

Tip checked a few other folders on either side of his mother's—Derrick and Delton—but both of them were intact, papers in place. Only his mother's folder seemed to have been messed with. And it was obviously on purpose.

He locked everything up, then talked to the admin who oversaw the operation. "Who had access to the files on Holly Denton?" Tp asked.

"Anyone with general access," she said. "That means anyone above sergeant or anyone who had permission."

"Have you got a record on who looked at what files?"

"I've got a record on who took which files, but not who looked at them."

"So if someone wanted to come in here and take papers from a folder, they could put it in another folder and just walk out?"

"Absolutely."

Tip slammed his hand on the desk. "Goddamn!" he said.

"What's wrong?"

"Nothing," he said. "Forget I asked. And do me a favor, darlin'. Don't tell anyone I was here."

"You got it," Missy said. "Far as I know, you were never here."

WHAT'S IN THE REPORT?

It took only a few well-placed questions to discover that Officer Simms, from the Fourth Ward, had been one of the original investigators on his mother's case. Tip had even run into her while he patrolled the area. Monday morning, he used some free time and went to see her.

He found her on Navigation, near the original Ninfa's. He pulled up to the curb and rolled the window down. "Simms, you got a minute?"

She looked over at him, must have recognized him, then waved. "Denton, that you? Haven't seen you since you graduated from the academy."

"Some of us get lucky," I guess. "Which brings me to a question. Did you work the Holly Denton case about twenty years ago?"

"Why do you want to know?" She seemed skeptical.

"She was my mother."

Simms nodded. "I wondered, with the same last name but I didn't want to ask. Yeah, I worked that case along with Richardson, but he's retired now."

Tip got out of the car and leaned against the side. "I went looking for the files last week, and imagine my surprise when I found the folder empty."

Simms shook her head. "Doesn't surprise me. Somebody wanted that case hushed up. I pushed it when I had it, and that's what earned me the demotion to Officer Simms instead of Detective Simms."

"Are you shittin' me?" Tip asked.

"Not about that," she said. "I've been trying to claw my way out of here ever since. I'm sure they want me to quit, but I'm not going to do it."

"What about your partner?"

"Like I said, retired. I'm betting it was forced retirement, but that's probably a gift for him shutting his mouth. He never told."

"Told what?"

"I shouldn't say."

"Forget *shouldn't*. Tell me what you know. This is my mother we're talking about."

Simms looked around, as if someone might be watching. "We found a Ranger's badge on her body."

Tip looked at her as if she had spoken Greek. "Ranger's badge? What the hell does that mean?"

"Guess you're too young to know. Back then, there was a spate of killings all marked with the same signature—the badge of a Texas Ranger. All the other killings were high rollers, people of power or money. Your mother was the only one who broke the mold. Far as we could tell, whoever did this was a pro, a hitman."

"What? Who would want her dead? She was a goddamn waitress. Who would pay to have a waitress killed?"

"Did you know she'd had an abortion?" Simms asked.

"What? No! No way. She wasn't pregnant."

Simms nodded. "Yeah, she was. Her friend and co-worker even told us."

"Son of a bitch," Tip said. "Sally said she was pregnant? I didn't even know."

"I'm figuring you weren't old enough to know," Simms said. "My guess is that she got hooked up with the wrong person, got pregnant, and then had an abortion. But I have no idea why the son of a bitch would kill her. If she didn't have the abortion, okay, but why kill her if she got rid of the baby?"

"Son of a bitch," Tip said. "What else did you find out?"

"Not much. We had one witness who said the killer might have driven a light-blue pickup. Other than that—and a generic description—nothing."

"So why'd they bust you and not Richardson?"

"Orders had come down from the top not to report on the badge. I ignored that. Richardson didn't."

"What about the other Ranger killings?"

"No idea. Never had a chance to look into them. This happened too fast. I'm telling you, it goes way up, because somebody with juice had me transferred right after the report was filed. Somebody didn't want us looking into it."

"Why'd you do it, then?"

"Like I told Richardson way back, I signed up to solve crimes, not hide them. If that puts me in the Fourth Ward, so be it. I've been doing some good."

Tip reached over and hugged her. "Simms, you're okay. I like you."

"That makes two of us," she said.

"All right," Tip said. "I'm gonna keep looking into this. I'll let you know if I find anything."

"Good luck," Simms said. "Just watch your ass or you'll end up back here—or dead."

"I don't think it's that bad."

Simms nodded. "Trust me. Don't underestimate the danger."

WHO KILLED HOLLY DENTON?

Tip wanted to heed the advice Simms had given him, but he also *had* to find out who killed his mother. That one question had been on his mind for twenty years. He wasn't going to let it fester any longer.

With his mind made up, Tip decided to take things slow and careful. He restricted knowledge of his visits to the graveyard to Missy, and he only visited late at night. He also swore Missy to secrecy. He felt he could trust her because he'd gone through the academy with her brother and had gotten to know her family well.

After two years, and dozens of midnight trips to the graveyard, he'd found nothing new. No papers on his mother and nothing that mentioned the Ranger, despite Simms telling Tip that there'd been several previous murders attributed to the Ranger.

Tip was at a dead end and he didn't want to be, nor could he afford to be. He had to find out who did this and why. He made a decision that he'd go see Richardson, find out what he knew that Simms didn't. Richardson might not have been willing to stand up for what was right back then, but that was twenty years ago, and besides, retirement had a way of mellowing people out.

Tip found out where Richardson lived and stopped by on his way home. He knocked on the door and waited. A moment later, a middle-aged man, with graying hair answered. He was smiling and his eyes shone brightly.

"Can I help you?"

Tip showed his badge. "I'm Officer Tip Denton with the HPD. Twenty years ago you and Detective Simms investigated the death of Holly Denton; she was my mother."

Richardson lost his smile and narrowed his eyes. "Can't help you," he said, and started to close the door.

Tip wedged his foot between the door jamb and the door. "I think you can," he said. Then he pushed the door open and stepped inside. "And I think you will. She was my mother, and I intend to find out who killed her."

Richardson stumbled when Tip shoved the door open. He quickly recovered, holding on to the railing by the stairs. "What do you want? I don't know anything."

"I want what you know, whether you think you know anything or not."

Richardson walked into the living room and sat in a stiff, straight-backed chair. "What I know ain't much."

Tip took a seat on the sofa opposite him. "I'm sure it's more than I know. Start with the witnesses."

"There was only one witness, a customer at the diner. He was in his car when it went down."

Tip was busy taking notes while Richardson talked.

"I'm sure Simms must have told you this already. She's been dying to break this case since it happened."

"And you weren't?" Tip asked.

"I wanted to solve it, but some others didn't, and they had a lot more juice."

"Who were they?"

"Have no idea, and wouldn't tell you if I did know. I'm living off retirement now, and it wouldn't take much for them to mess that up. I don't intend to give up my retirement for a twenty-year-old case."

"If that case was about your mother, you would."

"Well, it ain't about my mother, so move on. Next question."

Tip tensed. He felt like punching the guy, but he held his temper, opting to squeeze his fist instead. "You got the witness's name?"

Richardson shook his head. "Never did have it. He called his statement in from a flyer Simms put out. He wouldn't say who he was."

"What did he tell you?"

"Like Simms probably told you already, that the guy got out of a blue pickup, walked over to your mother's car, got in and shot her. Then he got back in his truck and left. He was white, maybe thirty, and medium build. That's all I know."

"And you got no other leads on her or the Ranger?"

"Nothing on her. As far as the Ranger, we never got that far. Simms was re-assigned and I retired."

"That's pretty young to retire."

"I had my time in."

"And why did Simms go to the streets?"

"You'd have to ask her. I have no idea."

"So that's it? Twenty years and you're still afraid to talk? It must be hard living like this?"

"I eat. I drink a few beers. And I got a place to sleep. Can't ask for too much more."

Tip stood and walked toward the front door. "Like I said, must be hard."

During the next week, Tip talked to Simms twice, but all she did was admonish him for talking and confirming her previous statements—as well as Richardson's.

On Thursday, Tip was called in to the lieutenant's office. "What's up?" he asked.

"Have a seat, Denton."

He sat in the chair opposite him and stared.

"We have several complaints against you. One for police brutality and one for sexual harassment."

"Bullshit! Who said so?"

"I can't say who, but the brutality isn't even by the person you abused. It's a bystander who witnessed it."

Tip jumped up and pointed at the lieutenant. "That's a goddamn lie. I never touched anybody."

"Sit down, Denton. And it's not a lie according to these reports."

"Yeah, and I'd bet your uncle's ass they're both anonymous, aren't they?"

"I can't tell you who they're from, and it doesn't matter. Why would someone taint your reputation with false allegations?"

"Exactly. That's what I want to know."

"Have you got reason to suspect someone?"

"I've got plenty of reason, but I don't know who to suspect." Then Tip told the lieutenant about the personal investigation into his mother's murder and the connection to the Ranger badge and what happened to the original detectives.

The lieutenant shook his head slowly. "I don't know if I believe you, Denton, but I don't believe the brutality charge. That alone makes me want to dismiss this, but my hands are tied. As of last week, all brutality complaints go to the captain, and he has a policy that they all come with suspension until they are resolved. So like it or not, you're getting suspended."

"Son of a bitch!" Tip said.

"Yeah, either way it's a son of a bitch. But if you think that what you're saying is true, you'd better be quiet about it. Take your punishment and forget the whole thing happened. That's what I would do."

"What *is* going to happen?"

"You're suspended without pay until I can figure this out."

Tip stood and stared at the lieutenant. "It's easy to say forget the whole thing happened for you, but it wasn't your mother who was killed."

A NEW JOB

Two weeks went, by and still nothing was resolved. The brutality charges had not been dropped. Neither had the sexual harassment charges. He did find out that those had supposedly came from a clerk at the DMV. Another lie. And once again, Tip wondered who was behind this and why.

As he was pondering his future, he got word that Aunt Sally had been in a car accident. He went to the hospital to see her but she was in a coma—neurological damage. When he asked what happened, he discovered her car had been hit by a garbage truck that had apparently run a stop light. Tip lowered his head and shook it. Sally's *accident* was too much of a coincidence. *Somebody* was tying up loose ends.

Regardless, Tip had to put a stop to this; Simms had family. He wasn't going to be responsible for them getting hurt.

He got to the station at eight o'clock and went to see the lieutenant.

"What do you need, Denton?"

Tip handed him a paper. "I'm submitting my resignation."

"Resignation? You giving up, Denton?"

"Not giving up, but putting things on hold."

"You sure you want to do this?"

"I'm sure," Tip said. "If there's one thing my mama taught me, it was to carry your own weight, and I've been letting others do it for me. That's gonna stop."

"Suit yourself," the lieutenant said. "But if you change your mind, you have until the end of the day to let me know."

"I won't, but thanks." Tip shook hands and walked out of the office. He stopped at a nearby coffee shop on his way home. Officer John Renkin was seated at the counter.

"Renkin, haven't seen you in a while," Tip said.

Renkin turned on the stool and shook hands. "Has been a while, Denton. Since we crossed paths in the Fourth."

"The good old days," Tip said.

Renkin laughed. "I don't know if I'd call them good, but they *were* interesting. What have you been up to?"

"I just quit," Tip said. "Effective today."

"What? Why?"

Tip looked around, then grabbed Renkin by the shoulder. "Let's go over here. It's more private."

Renkin picked up his coffee and joined Tip at the table. "Now, tell me what the hell is going on."

Tip leaned forward and told him everything, then sat up straight. "That's all of it, John. I can't fight what I don't know."

"You need to come with me," Renkin said. "I'm moving to the County."

"What? The County?"

"Damn right. And they're giving me a promotion to boot. Put in your application and I'll make sure you get in, and maybe even get with me."

Tip thought about it, but only for a moment. "Deal," he said. "I'll drop by there tomorrow."

Renkin put his hand out to shake. "Goddamn, it's gonna be good to work together again."

"Goddamn if it won't," Tip said. "But I'm not gonna stop working my mom's case."

"No need to. No matter how far up this goes, they're not gonna fire us both. Besides, unless the juice goes real high, we're safe at county."

"But they might kill us."

"Let them try," Renkin said. "I've dealt with my share of crackers."

Tip took a sip of his drink, then looked at Renkin. "John, I greatly appreciate this and I won't forget it. I'm gonna find the son of a bitch who killed my mama, and then I'm gonna—"

"Don't go there, Tip. I don't want to know what you'll do. Do what you have to when it happens but don't tell me about it. Deal?"

Tip reached out and shook Renkin's hand again. "Goddamn, I'm glad I stopped by here. We're gonna have fun working together."

Renkin stood, gulped down the last of his coffee, then slapped Tip on the shoulder. "You got it, Denton. See ya later."

THE END OF THE STORY

"So that's the story, huh?" Connie asked.

"That's it," Tip said. "Now you know as much as I do."

"Which isn't much. How about Simms or the witness? Or Richardson?"

"Simms is retired now. I never found the witness, and Richardson is still mute. I tried him a couple of times."

"So all you know is, it was supposedly an average white guy driving a blue pickup?"

"That's about the size of it. But I'm not done looking. Somebody, somewhere, knows about this. And I'm gonna find them. I learned a long time ago that the best way to hunt was to listen, and I got ears all over the streets. Sooner or later, one of them will hear something."

"And I plan on helping you," Connie said. "We'll find this guy together."

Tip laughed. "You're a saucy gal. If I didn't know any better, I'd swear you were from New York."

"Tip, I got news for you. I *am* from New York. Brooklyn is *in* New York."

"I'll be a son of a bitch," Tip said. "I guess I missed the geography class when they taught that."

"I'm guessin' you missed a lot of classes, Tip. No matter, though. We don't need a formal education to find this prick. We'll get him."

Tip leaned over and kissed her on the cheek. "Thanks, Connie. My mom would have appreciated this."

Connie pulled out of the parking lot and turned left. "You want shitty coffee or pissy coffee?"

"I'd rather have good coffee."

"At this time of night, that's not an option. So which is it?"

"I guess I'll go with shitty coffee," Tip said.

"Good. I know just the place," Connie said, then they both laughed.

ALSO BY GIACOMO GIAMMATTEO

Non-Fiction:

No Mistakes Resumes, Book I of No Mistakes Careers

No Mistakes Interviews, Book II of No Mistakes Careers

No Mistakes Grammar, Volume I, Misused Words

No Mistakes Writing, Volume I—Writing Shortcuts

Uneducated

Fiction:

Friendship & Honor Series:

Murder Takes Time

Murder Has Consequences

Murder Takes Patience

Blood Flows South Series:

A Bullet For Carlos: A Connie Gianelli Mystery

Finding Family, a Novella

A Bullet From Dominic

Redemption Series:

Necessary Decisions: A Gino Cataldi Mystery

Old Wounds

Promises Kept, the Story of Number Two

Other Books Coming Soon

Fiction

A Promise of Vengeance (Fantasy)

My first fantasy, and the first book in a four-book series—the Rules of Vengeance. (Three are already written and the fourth is being outlined.)

Murder Is Invisible ### (going through editing)

Frankie and Nicky are back.

Premeditated, Redemption IV

A Hard Life, the Story of Tip Denton

Non-Fiction

No Mistakes Grammar, Volume III, More Misused Words. (being proofread)

Whiskers and Bear—Volume I of the Life on the Farm Series (sent to editor)

No Mistakes Publishing, How to Self-Publish a Book

No Mistakes Writing, How to Write a Bestseller

Children's Books

No Mistakes Grammar for Kids, Volume I—Much and Many (Sent to editor)

No Mistakes Grammar for Kids, Volume II—Lie and Lay (Sent to editor)

No Mistakes Grammar for Kids, Volume III—Then and Than (Sent to editor)

Shinobi Goes to School—Life on the Farm for kids. (working on illustrations)

Get on the mailing list and you'll be sure to be notified of release dates and sales.

[Mailing list](#)

And don't forget to leave a review!

ABOUT THE AUTHOR

Giacomo Giammatteo is the author of gritty crime dramas about murder, mystery, and family. He also writes non-fiction books including the No Mistakes Careers series.

When Giacomo isn't writing, he's helping his wife take care of the animals on their sanctuary. At last count they had 45 animals—11 dogs, a horse, 6 cats, and 26 pigs.

Oh, and one crazy—and very large—wild boar, who takes walks with Giacomo every day and happens to also be his best buddy.

giacomogiammatteo.com
gg@giacomog.com

ACKNOWLEDGMENTS

Special thanks to my sister Rose and my daughter-in-law, Missy, for being consistent and helpful beta readers. It's not hard to be honest with feedback, but they always are.

Printed by Libri Plureos GmbH in Hamburg, Germany